SANTA MARIA PUBLIC LIBRARY

D0535128

j618.4   Parent Shelf

Rosenberg, Maxine B.
    Mommy's in the Hospital Having
   Baby.

Mommy's in the Hospital Having a Baby

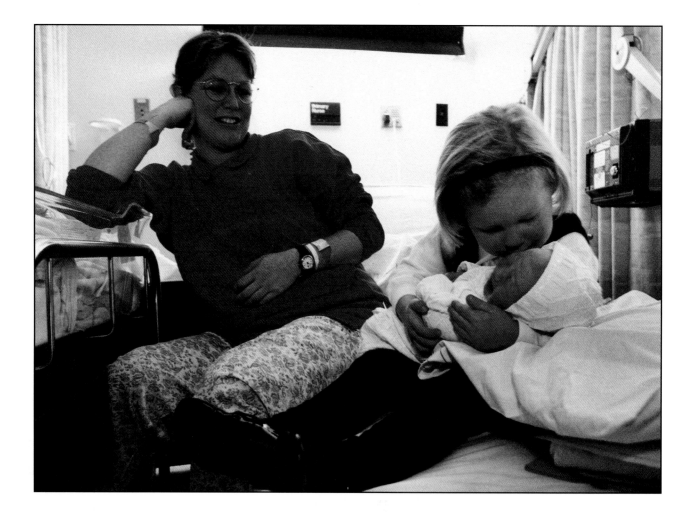

Mommy's in the Hospital Having a Baby

by Maxine B. Rosenberg
Photographs by Robert Maass

CLARION BOOKS
New York

*To Gina Maccoby, who smoothes out
the wrinkles
—M.B.R.*

Acknowledgments

The author and photographer wish to thank Beth Israel Hospital in Manhattan for generously allowing them to use the facility. Special thanks also go to Karen Rubin, the coordinator of parent education at the hospital who made the project that much easier. The author too is grateful to Jean Schopell at New York Hospital for letting her join the sibling tour and listen to the wonderful comments of the children.

Clarion Books
a Houghton Mifflin Company imprint
215 Park Avenue South, New York, NY 10003
Text copyright © 1997 by Maxine B. Rosenberg
Photographs copyright © 1997 by Robert Maass
Book design by Carol Goldenberg
Text is 18/22-point Cheltenham ITC Book

All rights reserved.
For information about permission to reproduce selections from this book,
write to Permissions, Houghton Mifflin Company,
215 Park Avenue South, New York, NY 10003.

For information about this and other Houghton Mifflin trade and reference books
and multimedia products, visit The Bookstore at Houghton Mifflin on the World Wide Web
at (http://www.hmco.com/trade/).

Printed in China.

Library of Congress Cataloging-in-Publication Data
Rosenberg, Maxine B.
Mommy's in the hospital having a baby / by Maxine B. Rosenberg ; photographs by Robert Maass.
p.   cm.
Summary: Describes the care that mothers and babies receive in the hospital and tells children
what to expect if they go to visit their new brother or sister.
ISBN 0-395-71813-9
1. Childbirth—Juvenile literature.   2. Hospitals, Gynecologic and obstetric—Juvenile literature.
3. Hospitals—Nurseries—Juvenile literature.   4. Infants (Newborn)—Juvenile literature.
5. Brothers and sisters—Juvenile literature.   [1. Babies.   2. Hospitals.   3. Brothers and sisters.]
I. Maass, Robert, ill.   II. Title.
RG525.5.R68   1997
618.4—dc20   96-12442
CIP
AC

TPC   10   9   8   7   6   5   4   3   2   1

Note to Parents

Today more and more hospitals are allowing siblings to visit their mothers on the maternity floor. It's not unusual to see children as young as two years old in the halls, in front of the nursery window, and even in their mothers' rooms.

Years back, siblings were kept away from newborns to prevent the babies from contracting communicable diseases. But with little evidence of healthy siblings spreading infection, they're now being welcomed to the maternity floor.

To acquaint children with this part of the hospital, sibling classes are often held. A month or two before the baby is due, small groups of children accompanied by one or both parents are taken on a tour led by an obstetrics nurse. Siblings are encouraged to ask questions and express their feelings toward the new baby.

It's important for children to be prepared for the upcoming birth and to understand what will be happening while their mothers are away. The more they're reassured that their mothers and they themselves will be well taken care of during this time, the less anxious they'll be. And the sooner they feel part of the new family, the smoother their transition to becoming a big brother/big sister.

2

*S*omething important is about to happen in your family. Your mommy is having a baby.

She'll go to a hospital where the baby will be born.

When Mommy is in the hospital, she'll stay on the maternity floor. That part of the hospital is just for moms and new babies. There are no sick people on the maternity floor.

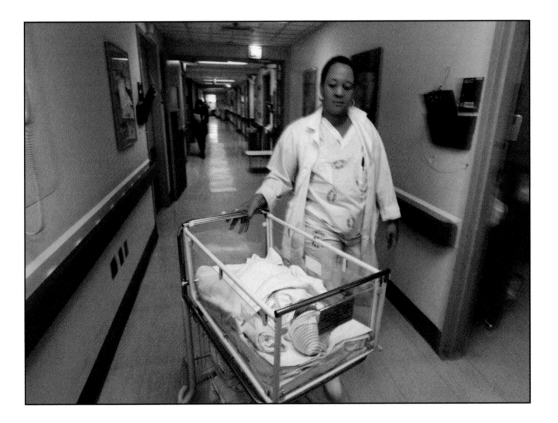

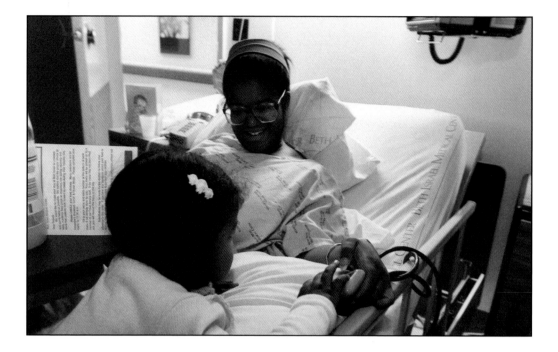

Mommy will be very tired after having the baby. She'll need plenty of rest. She'll want to relax in her special hospital bed. It has many buttons.

One button makes the bed go up high so the nurse won't hurt her back when she bends over to change the sheets. Another button makes the bed go down low so Mom can climb in and out easily. There are also buttons to raise the front and back of the bed. Without moving, Mom can put her feet up high and read a book. Or she can press a button to turn on the T.V.

If you visit Mom, she might let you press a button and give her a ride.

In the hospital Mommy won't have to do any work. She won't even have to cook. All her meals will be prepared in the hospital kitchen. An aide will bring her food on a tray and Mom can eat it in bed. If she needs an extra pillow or wants the air conditioner turned up or down, an aide or a nurse will take care of that, too.

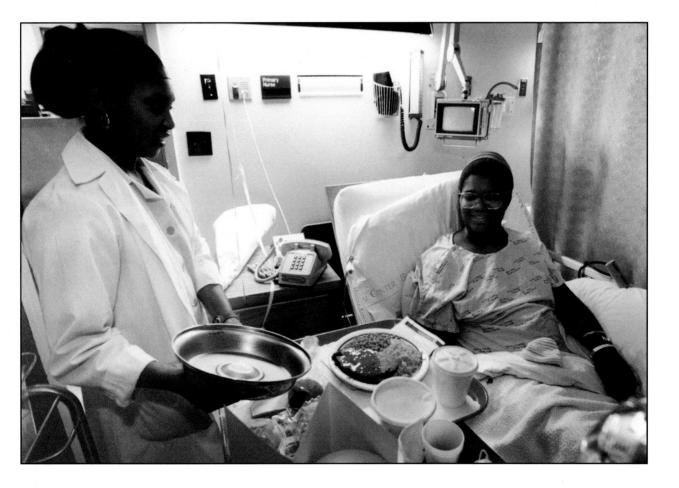

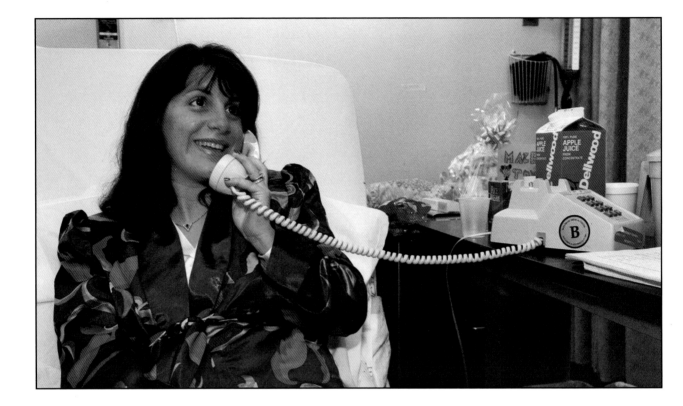

Of course, she'll miss you and want to talk to you and hear about your day. She'll use the telephone that's next to her bed to call you.

"Hi, sweetie," she'll say. "Did you have fun in the playground?"

You can call Mom too. Ask Dad or another grownup who's taking care of you to dial Mom's hospital telephone number.

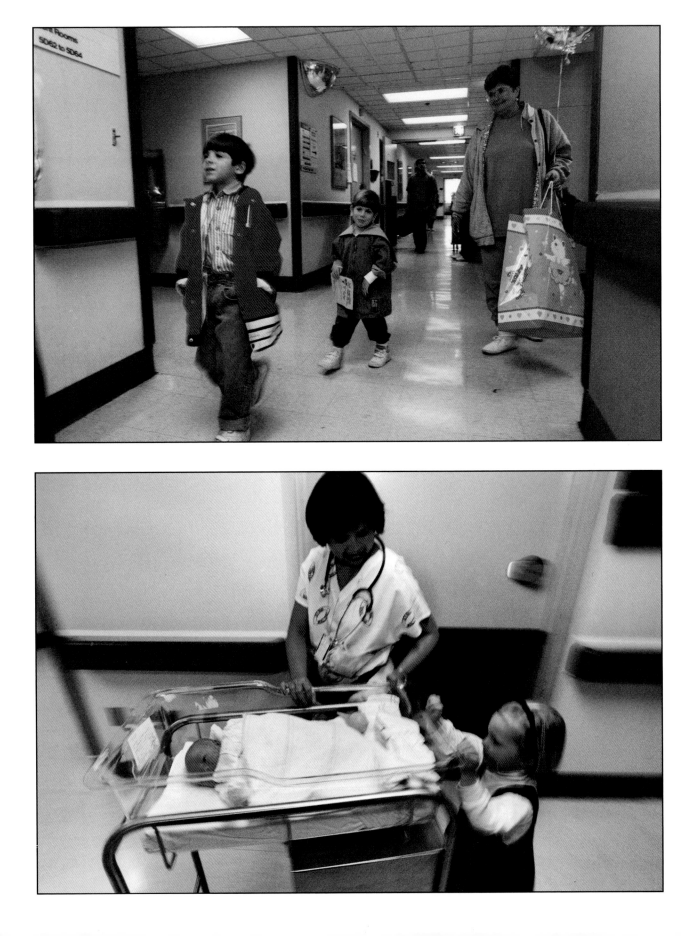

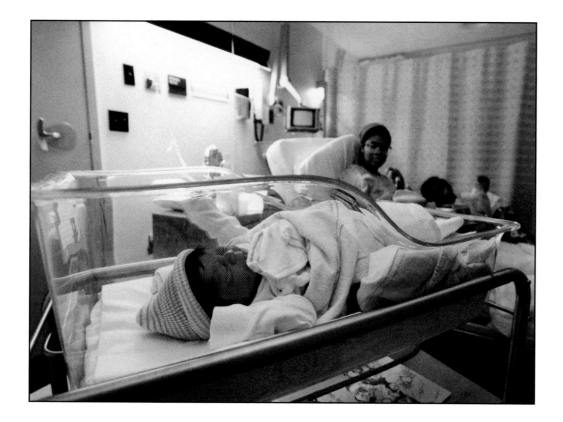

Some hospitals let children visit their parents. If Mom's hospital says you can see her there, you'll be so excited. You'll want to run into her arms and give her a big kiss. But hospital floors can be slippery, so remember to walk slowly. Otherwise you might fall or bump into a food cart.

You will also need to talk softly in the hospital so you won't wake up the babies and the other moms who are taking naps.

The new babies stay in the nursery and each sleeps in a little plastic crib that's on a rolling cart. Above each baby's head is a pink or blue card. Pink is for girls and blue is for boys. The card shows how much each baby weighed at birth. It has the baby's last name on it so the nurse knows which baby belongs to which mom.

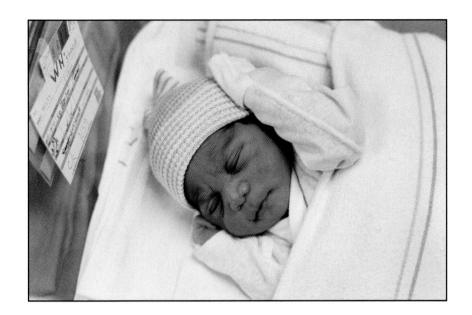

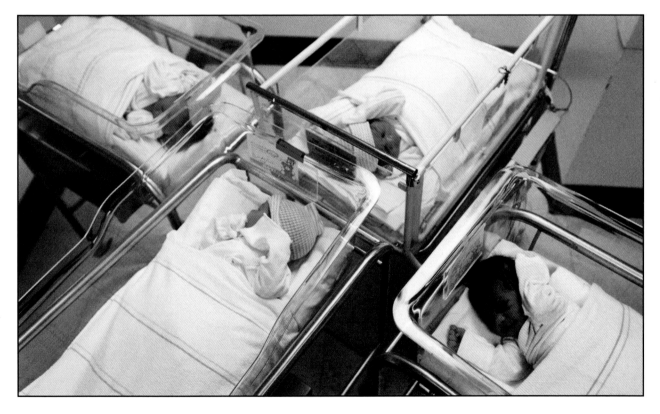

When Mom or Dad tells the nurse the baby's name, the nurse will wheel the baby's crib to the window. Then you'll see your new brother or sister up close.

The baby will be covered with a blanket and might be wearing a little hat. The hospital wants to make sure the baby is kept warm and snuggly, the way it was inside Mommy's body.

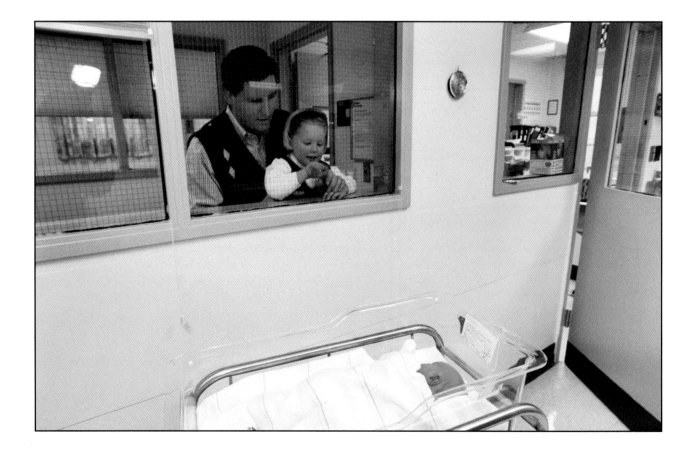

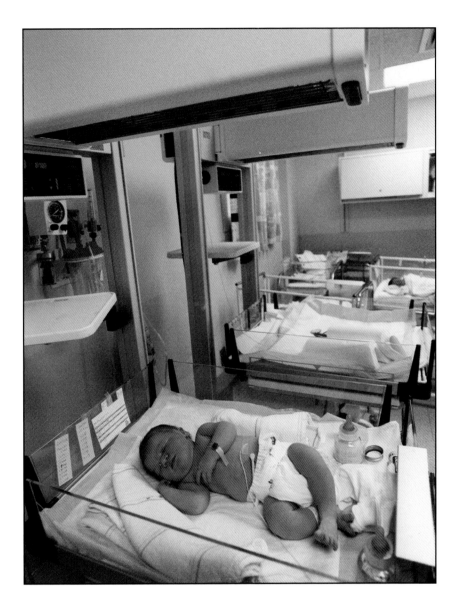

Some babies are chilly even with a blanket and hat, so the nurse puts them under warming lights until their bodies feel nice and toasty.

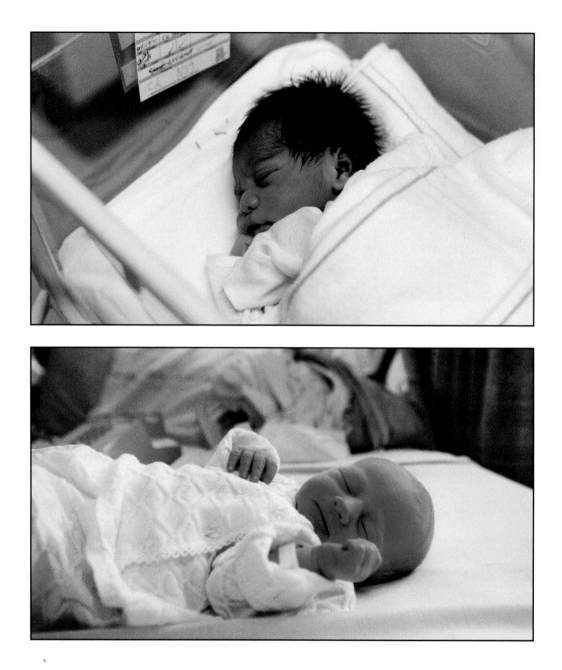

Every baby is different. Some have lots of hair and others are bald. Some keep their eyes tightly shut while others take a peek around.

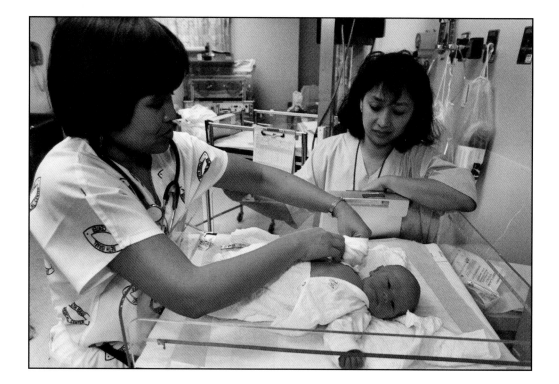

You'll see the different kinds of babies through the nursery window. If a nurse is changing a baby, you'll notice a funny little thing sticking out of the baby's belly button. It's called the umbilical cord. That's the tube that attached the baby to the mommy while inside her. The baby's food came through that tube.

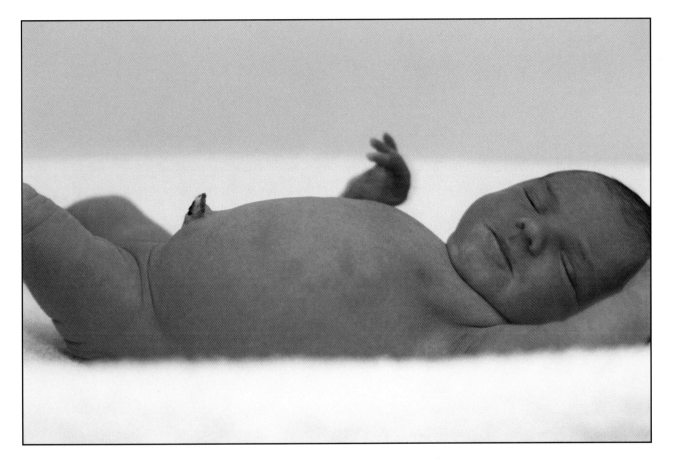

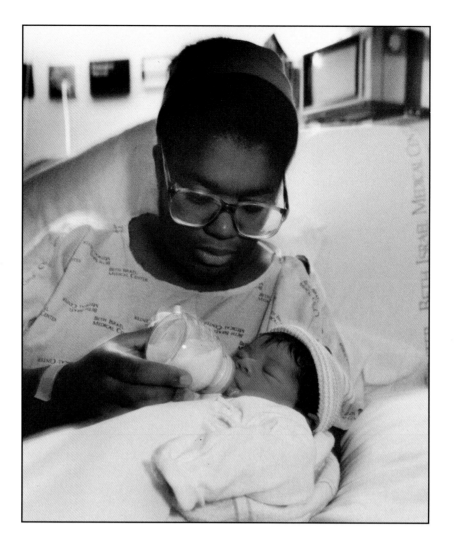

Once the baby is born, the baby's food comes from a bottle or the mother's breast, and the baby doesn't need the umbilical cord anymore.

The doctor cuts most of it off, which doesn't hurt the baby. In a few days, the small piece of cord remaining next to the baby's tummy dries up and falls off. What's left is the belly button.

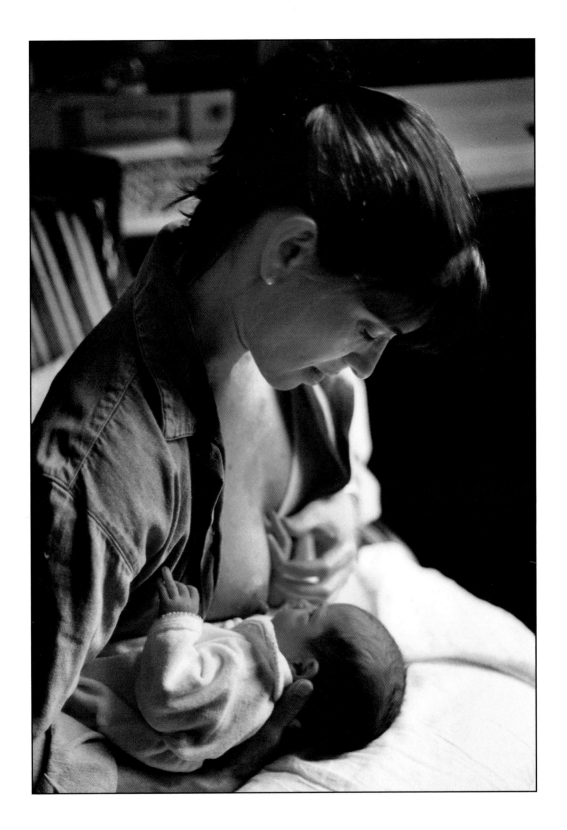

21

In the hospital the babies wear little bracelets on their ankles or wrists. These are name tags to prevent the nurses from getting the babies mixed up when taking them out of their cribs to feed or bath them, or while wheeling them into their mothers' rooms.

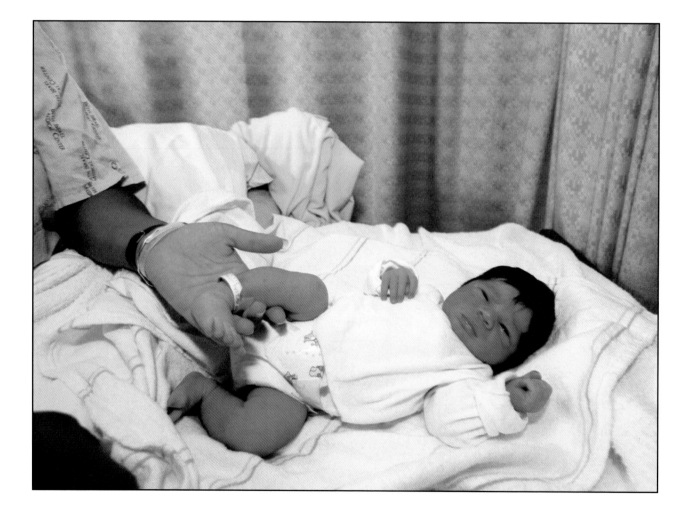

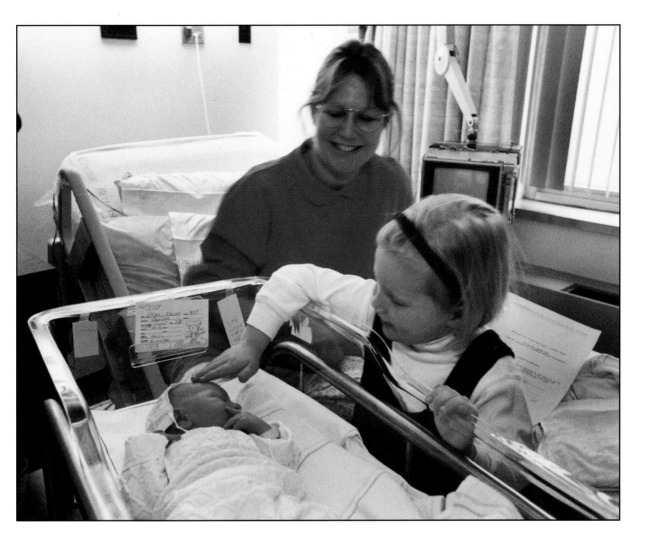

The babies are brought to their mothers' rooms several times a day. Maybe Mom's hospital will let you be in the room while your baby is there. Then you can gently touch your new brother or sister.

You can even hold the baby. Mom or Dad will show you how to cradle the baby's head so it doesn't wobble around.

Mom and Dad are going to need your help with the baby. You can bring a diaper when the baby needs changing. And you can hand them the bottle if the baby wants a drink. You'll think of other ways to help your mom and dad take care of the baby.

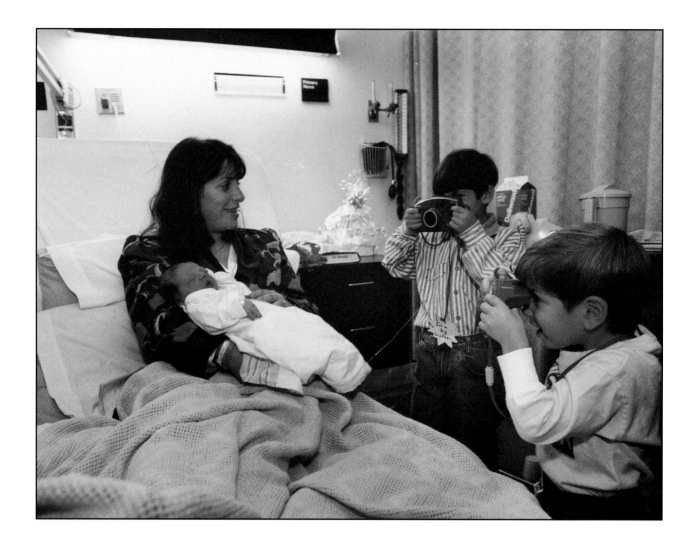

Mom will soon come home from the hospital. You'll be happy to have her nearby again, and she'll be happy to be home.

With a new baby in the house, you'll be a new kind of family. As the older brother or sister, you'll have lots of things to teach the baby that you've learned since you were a baby not so long ago.